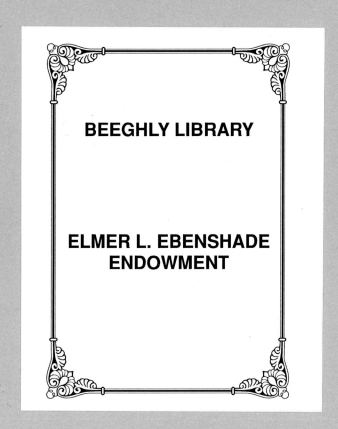

BOOKS BY ASHLEY BRYAN

Walk Together Children: Black American Spirituals
The Dancing Granny
Beat the Story-Drum, Pum-Pum
I'm Going to Sing: Black American Spirituals, Vol. II
The Cat's Purr
Lion and the Ostrich Chicks and other African Tales

THE DANCING GRANNY

Love

Ashley Bryan

The Dancing Granny

Retold and Illustrated by

Ashley Bryan

Aladdin Paperbacks

Aladdin Paperbacks
An imprint of Simon & Schuster
Children's Publishing Division
1230 Avenue of the Americas
New York, NY 10020

First Aladdin Books edition 1987
Printed in the United States of America

10 9 8 7 6 5 4

Library of Congress Cataloging-in-Publication Data
Bryan, Ashley.
The dancing granny.
Summary: Spider Ananse gets Granny started dancing
so he can raid her garden, but his own trick does him in.
1. Anansi (Legendary character) [1. Anansi (Legendary
character) 2. Folklore—West Indies] I. Title.
PZ8.1.B838Dan   1987   398.2'452'544 [E]   87-1140
ISBN 0-689-71149-2

To the memory of
GRANNY SARAH BRYAN
and for her Great-Granddaughters
VERNA RAI AND BARI JAN

"The music sweet me so."

THE DANCING GRANNY

THERE WAS AN OLD WOMAN who lived in a hut. Everyone called her Granny Anika.

She sang her songs and she stirred her pot. She licked the ladle and tasted her stew. Umm-yum! She beat the sides of the calabash, pom-pa-lom! pom-pa-lom!

Granny Anika was a happy old lady. She woke up singing. All day long she sang and beat out rhythms on anything within reach. She rapped with sticks, she drummed with spoons, she tapped with ladles and she hummed dance tunes to the beat of her knives.

"Shake it to the East,
Shake it to the West."

But what Granny Anika loved best of all was to dance. She danced in the morning. She danced at noon. She danced till the sun set. And then at night she dreamed dance dreams and danced in her sleep till dawn.

That old lady was never too busy or tired to do a
little dance. She cleared a vegetable patch near her
hut and sang as she hoed the ground. She kept step
to the chop, chop, chop of her hoe.

The seeds stirred in the earth to the vibrations of Granny's song and dance. The vegetables came up strong to the gentle slap, pitter-pat of Old Anika's bare feet.

Granny Anika was proud of her grounds. She set in a good variety of seeds and raised all of her provisions. She sang:

"*Mama loves peas,*
Papa loves corn,
Baby loves beans
Sure as you're born.
Put in potatoes,
Granny loves yam,
Don't forget okra,
Beets and jam."

Jam! Well, Granny picked sweet berries from bushes and made a thick brew, which she spread on sliced yam and called jam.

Granny Anika did her share of work, and she did her dance. Uh-huh! She snapped her fingers and clapped her hands. Uh-huh! She knew her song, and she got along.

Uh-huh!

One day Spider Ananse came strutting on by Granny Anika's hut.

You couldn't imagine a lazier fellow than Brother Ananse. He'd strut and stroll all day long, looking like he was doing something important. But Spider wouldn't work.

No kind of tune could make the hoe feel lighter in Brother Ananse's hands. And no kind of beat eased his long, slim feet on a spade dug into the ground.

Spider Ananse preferred resting and loafing and lounging and wandering around until he found someone he might trick for his dinner.

Spider watched Granny Anika working in her field. She was bent over the hoe doing a jig as she dug. She didn't see Spider Ananse climb into a tree.

Spider Ananse peeped out at Granny from behind the tree trunk. "Hmm . . ." he thought, "I won't get a thing from that great garden patch if Granny doesn't go."

Brother Ananse began to sing. He sang one of his catchiest tunes. He broke off a twig and rapped out a marked dance beat on a dead branch.

> "Pom-pa-lom!
> Pom-pa-lom!
> Papa's here
> And Mama's gone.
> I sing, you dance, my dee-dee.
> You dance, I sing, my swee-tee.
> I'll trouble you, my dee-dee,
> I'll trouble you, my la-dy."

Granny heard the tune and hummed it to herself.
"Umm-hmm! Sweet, sweet, sweet," she sang.

Then the music and the beat got to Granny's feet.
She held her hoe like a partner and swung with it
to the right. She swung to the left.

Spider Ananse sang out:

> *"Shake it to the East,*
> *Shake it to the West.*
> *Shake it to the very one*
> *That you love the best."*

Granny Anika skipped like a little girl. She flung
out her arms, dropping the hoe, and danced off the
field.

Spider Ananse sang louder and louder and rapped harder and harder.

Granny Anika wheeled to the East. She wheeled to the West. She let the music take her, and the dance carried her off. Away she wheeled northwards, head over heels, until she disappeared from sight.

Then Brother Ananse dropped down from the tree laughing till he shook.

"There goes the dancing Granny." He laughed. "Man! She sure looked like a tumbleweed as she wheeled by."

Spider helped himself to all the corn he could
carry and carted it off to his house.

His wife said, "Good corn."

His mother said, "Sure as you're born."

That night they all sat down to heaping platefuls
of steaming corn.

When Granny Anika finally came out of her dance right side up, she was eleven miles north of her village.

"O my! O my!" she cried. "I know that voice. It was Brother Ananse. He sure can sing. Now why didn't he come dance with me? Anyway, I got a good dance to the North."

Back home, Granny went to her field and saw that her corn crop was ravished.

"Eh, eh! That good-for-nothing, no' count Spider Ananse! He sure tricked me. So, that's why he didn't try to match my steps! But I'll catch him. Next time he comes I won't let the music sweet me so."

Sure enough, Spider Ananse soon came round
again to plunder Granny's vegetable patch.

"Umm-yum," he thought as he looked out over the pretty field. "If the corn tasted so good, I wonder how Granny's peas and beans might be."

Spider Ananse climbed into the tree and began to sing:

> *"Ah mini lah lee lee*
> *Again I'm in the country*
> *'Cause Nana's corn*
> *Tastes good to me.*
> *I see those beans,*
> *I see those greens,*
> *I see those beets,*
> *Fit for kings and queens."*

"See what you see and see what you like and have a fit too," said Granny, "'cause that see and that fit is all you're going to get. You can sing for beans and sing for peas for all I care. It's going to take two to dance to your tune today." Granny shuffled her feet lightly. "Yeah! Take a good look. You'll see that your Mama lives right here, and she don't plan to go nowhere. Uh-uh, no wheres away. Not this here day."

Spider laughed and did some variations on his rapping. Then he went into his big song:

> *"Pom-pa-lom!*
> *Pom-pa-lom!*
> *Papa's here*
> *But Mama's gone.*
> *I sing for peas,*
> *I sing for corn.*
> *You plant, I'll pull,*
> *Sure as you're born."*

Granny Anika held her hoe tightly and dug her toes into the ground.

Spider sang on:

> "*I sing, you dance, my dee-dee.*
> *You dance, I sing, my swee-tee.*
> *I trouble you, my dee-dee,*
> *I trouble you, my la-dy.*'

Granny kicked up her feet and dropped the hoe.

Spider sang:

"O! Shake it to the East
Shake it to the West,
Shake it to the very one
That you love the best."

Granny's feet could no longer resist Spider's beat.
She wheeled to the East, she wheeled to the West.
Then head over heels, she cartwheeled southwards.

"Man, if Granny don't spin like a thistle on the breath of a whistle," laughed Spider, dropping out of the tree. He watched the dancing Granny twirl out of sight.

Then Spider filled his bag with peas and beans and strutted all the way home.

Spider's wife said, "Good beans, good peas."

Spider's mother said, "If you please."

That night they all sat down to heaping gourds of hot beans and peas.

Granny Anika found herself twelve miles south of her village before she danced Spider's tune out of her feet.

When she got back home, she saw that Spider
Ananse had stolen her peas and beans.

"How can I catch that thieving rascal?" she said.
"Brother Ananse sings the danciest tunes. I just
can't stay still when the music sweets me so. That I
know. Trouble is, Spider knows it too."

Spider Ananse came again and climbed into the tree. He stayed well out of reach of Granny, but his voice reached Granny Anika well.

"Put your hands on your hips
And let your backbone shake."

Once Spider got into his song, Granny couldn't resist. She danced to the North. She danced to the South. And when Spider sang the pom-pa-lom part, Granny was into her steps.

*"Shake it to the East,
Shake it to the West."*

Granny was now dancing her best and pleased as could be with her style. Even Spider Ananse had to admire her as she went, head over heels, cartwheeling westwards.

"That dancing Granny turns like a windmill!" he
exclaimed. "She sure can twirl her arms and legs in
time to the tune."

Spider took all the potatoes he could carry and toted the sack home.

Spider's wife said, "Good potatoes."

Spider's mother said, "Tastier than tomatoes."

That night they all sat down to a heaping mound of roasted potatoes.

Granny had a good dance, it's true. She came to a
stop thirteen miles to the west of her village and re-
turned home.

The fourth time Spider Ananse came by, he started singing before he was well into the tree.

"Pom-pa-lom!
Pom-pa-lom!
Papa's hungry
And Mama's not home."

Granny started her dance. She swayed to the South. She swayed to the North.

"Shake it to the East,
Shake it to the West."

"Sweet, sweet, sweet," sang Granny to the beat.

Spider didn't even have to finish his song. Granny heard well, and the tune was wheeling in her. Off she went, heels over head, wheeling eastwards.

Spider Ananse shook his head and said, "No one can outdance dancing Granny. She spins like a top."

He filled his basket with beets and beat it on back home.

Spider's wife said, "Good beets."

Spider's mother said, "Sweeter than sweets."

That night they all sat down to big bowls of boiled beets.

Granny Anika danced to a stop, right side up fourteen miles to the east of her village.

"My," she said, "that was the sweetest dance of all."

When she got home, Granny sat by her hut. She
tapped her foot as she looked out over her ravished
field.

"Look at that, will you?" she said. "Trickster
Spider's done taken my corn, my peas and beans,
my potatoes and my beets. I'll never catch that
clever character as long as he swings on that sweet
song."

So Granny Anika gathered in all that was left of
her vegetables. There was nothing more in the
fields for Brother Ananse to steal.

When Spider Ananse sauntered by again, he was so sure of himself that he started singing his song long before he reached the tree. Now what did he do that for?

Granny Anika was waiting for just such a chance. Quickly she swung her hoe and caught Brother Ananse around the waist. She pulled him to her and held onto him as if he were the first dance partner she ever had.

"Let go! Let go of me," Spider cried.

"I've got you now, you singing brother," said Granny. "Dance with me. To the East, to the West, to the North, to the South. Sing your song."

Granny Anika pinched Spider, and he began to
sing:

> "Pom-pa-lom!
> Pom-pa-lom!
> I ate your peas,
> I ate your corn."

"Sure as you're born, you did. Now dance,
Brother! Dance!" sang Granny to the song. "I'll
teach you that two can trip to that tune too."

Granny Anika led Spider Ananse in the dance.
They whirled and they twirled to the wheeling beat.
Every time Spider tried to stop, Granny squeezed
him tighter.

They danced to the North.
They danced to the South.

Now Spider's feet felt the sweet beat of Granny's
steps. Together they sang:

> *Shake it to the East,*
> *Shake it to the West,*
> *Shake it to the very one*
> *That you love the best."*

They wheeled to the East.
They whirled to the West.

They heeled to the North.
They twirled to the South.

Off they went capering and cartwheeling away!
Pom-pa-lom!
Pom-pa-lom!

Spider Ananse didn't get one vegetable from
Granny Anika that day, but he sure got one good
dance with the old woman.

Dancing Granny never had a better partner than
Spider Ananse. They danced more miles together
than Granny had ever danced alone. And if Spider's
still singing, then they're still dancing.

"Dance Granny! You move like the river."
"Dance Spider! Let's dance forever."
"Dance, Granny! As the lead bends
"The dance goes on, but the story ends."

Retold from "He Sings to Make the Old Woman Dance," (Antigua, English Antilles). In *Folk-Lore of the Antilles, French and English,* Part II by Elsie Clews Parsons. New York: American Folk-Lore Society, 1936, p. 314.